the LITTLE SOUL *and the* SUN

A Children's Parable
Adapted from *Conversations with God*

Neale Donald Walsch

Illustrated by Frank Riccio

HAMPTON ROADS
PUBLISHING COMPANY, INC.

For information write:

Hampton Roads Publishing
665 Third Street, Suite 400
San Francisco, CA 94107
www.hrpub.com

Library of Congress Catalog Card Number: 98-71734

ISBN 978-1-57174-087-8

Manufactured in China
MD
20

To my future grandchildren,
should there be any,
and to every Little Soul
awaiting birth.

You are our blessing
and our hope,
our innocence
and our joy,
our promise
and our evidence
of God's unending love.

—N.D.W.

To the Blinding Light

—F.R.

ONCE UPON NO TIME there was a Little Soul who said to God, "I know who I am!"

And God said, "That's wonderful! Who are you?"

And the Little Soul shouted, "I'm the Light!"

God smiled a big smile. "That's right!" God exclaimed. "You are the Light."

The Little Soul was so happy, for it had figured out what all the souls in the Kingdom were there to figure out. "Wow," said the Little Soul, "this is really cool!"

But soon, knowing who it was was not enough. The Little Soul felt stirrings inside, and now wanted to *be* who it was. And so the Little Soul went back to God (which is not a bad idea for all souls who want to be Who They Really Are) and said, "Hi, God! Now that I know Who I Am, is it okay for me to be it?"

And God said, "You mean you want to be Who You *Already Are?*"

"Well," replied the Little Soul, "it's one thing to know Who I Am, and another thing altogether to actually be it. I want to feel what it's like to *be* the Light!"

"But you already *are* the Light," God repeated, smiling again.

"Yes, but I want to see what that *feels* like!" cried the Little Soul.

"Well," said God with a chuckle, "I suppose I should have known. You always were the adventuresome one." Then God's expression changed. "There's only one thing. . ."

"What?" asked the Little Soul.

"Well, there is nothing else *but* the Light. You see, I created nothing but what you are; and so, there is no easy way for you to experience yourself as Who You Are, since there is nothing that you are not."

"Huh?" said the Little Soul, who was now a little confused.

"Think of it this way," said God. "You are like a candle in the Sun. Oh, you're there all right. Along with a million, ka-gillion other candles who make up the Sun. And the sun would not be the Sun without you.

Nay, it would be a sun without one of its candles. . .and that would not be the Sun at all; for it would not shine as brightly. Yet, how to know yourself as the Light when you are *amidst* the Light—that is the question."

"Well," the Little Soul perked up, "you're God. Think of something!"

Once more God smiled. "I already have," God said. "Since you cannot see yourself as the Light when you are *in* the Light, we'll surround you with darkness."

"What's darkness?" the Little Soul asked.

God replied, "It is that which you are not."

"Will I be afraid of the dark?" cried the Little Soul.

"Only if you choose to be." God answered. "There is nothing, really, to be afraid of, unless you decide that there is. You see, we are making it all up. We are pretending."

"Oh," said the Little Soul, and felt better already.

Then God explained that, in order to experience anything at all, the exact opposite of it will appear. "It is a great gift," God said, "because without it, you could not know what anything is like.

"You could not know Warm without Cold, Up without Down, Fast without Slow. You could not know Left without Right, Here without There, Now without Then.

"And so," God concluded, "when you are surrounded with darkness, do not shake your fist and raise your voice and curse the darkness.

"Rather be a Light unto the darkness, and don't be mad about it. Then you will know Who You Really Are, and all others will know, too. Let your Light so shine that everyone will know how special you are!"

"You mean it's okay to let others see how special I am?" asked the Little Soul.

"Of course!" God chuckled. "It's very okay! But remember, 'special' does not mean 'better.' Everybody is special, each in their own way! Yet many others have forgotten that. They will see that it is okay for them to be special only when you see that it is okay for you to be special."

"Wow," said the Little Soul, dancing and skipping and laughing and jumping with joy. "I can be as special as I want to be!"

"Yes, and you can start right now," said God, who was dancing and skipping and laughing right along with the Little Soul. "What part of *special* do you want to be?"

"What part of *special*?" the Little Soul repeated. "I don't understand."

"Well," God explained, "being the Light is being special, and being special has a lot of parts to it. It is special to be kind. It is special to be gentle. It is special to be creative. It is special to be patient. Can you think of any other ways it is special to be?"

The Little Soul sat quietly for a moment. "I can think of lots of ways to be special!" the Little Soul then exclaimed. "It is special to be helpful. It is special to be sharing. It is special to be friendly. It is special to be considerate of others!"

"Yes!" God agreed, "and you can be all of those things, or any part of *special* you wish to be, at any moment. That's what it means to be the Light."

"But why? Why would you do that?" the Little Soul asked. "You, who are a Being of such utter perfection! You, who vibrate with such a speed that it creates a Light so bright that I can hardly gaze upon you! What could cause you to want to slow down your vibration to such a speed that your bright Light would become dark and dense? What could cause you—who are so light that you dance upon the stars and move throughout the Kingdom with the speed of your thought—to come into my life and make yourself so heavy that you could do this bad thing?"

"Simple," the Friendly Soul said. "I would do it because I love you."

It was then that the Little Soul realized a large crowd had gathered. Souls had come from far and wide—from all over the Kingdom—for the word had gone forth that the Little Soul was having this extraordinary conversation with God, and everyone wanted to hear what they were saying.

Looking at the countless other souls gathered there, the Little Soul had to agree. None appeared less wonderful, less magnificent, or less perfect than the Little Soul itself. Such was the wonder of the souls gathered around, and so bright was their Light, that the Little Soul could scarcely gaze upon them.

"Who, then, to forgive?" asked God.

"Boy, this is going to be no fun at all!" grumbled the Little Soul. "I wanted to experience myself as One Who Forgives. I wanted to know what that part of *special* felt like."

And the Little Soul learned what it must feel like to be sad.

But just then a Friendly Soul stepped forward from the crowd. "Not to worry, Little Soul," the Friendly Soul said, "I will help you."

"You will?" the Little Soul brightened. "But what can you do?"

"Why, I can give you someone to forgive!"

"You can?"

"Certainly!" chirped the Friendly Soul. "I can come into your next lifetime and do something for you to forgive."

"I know what I want to be, I know what I want to be!" the Little Soul announced with great excitement. "I want to be the part of *special* called 'forgiving.' Isn't it special to be forgiving?"

"Oh, yes," God assured the Little Soul. "That is very special."

"Okay," said the Little Soul. "That's what I want to be. I want to be forgiving. I want to experience myself as that."

"Good," said God, "but there's one thing you should know."

The Little Soul was becoming a bit impatient now. It always seemed as though there were some complication.
"What is it?" the Little Soul sighed.

"There is no one to forgive."

"No one?" The Little Soul could hardly believe what had been said.

"No one!" God repeated. "Everything I have made is perfect. There is not a single soul in all creation less perfect than you. Look around you."

The Little Soul seemed surprised at the answer.

"Don't be so amazed," said the Friendly Soul, "you have done the same thing for me. Don't you remember? Oh, we have danced together, you and I, many times. Through the eons and across all the ages have we danced. Across all time and in many places have we played together. You just don't remember.

"We have both been All Of It. We have been the Up and the Down of it, the Left and the Right of it. We have been the Here and the There of it, the Now and the Then of it. We have been the male and the female, the good and the bad—we have both been the victim and the villain of it.

"Thus have we come together, you and I, many times before; *each* bringing to the *other* the exact and perfect opportunity to Express and to Experience Who We Really Are.

"And so," the Friendly Soul explained a little further, "I will come into your next lifetime and be the 'bad one' this time. I will do something really terrible, and then you can experience yourself as the One Who Forgives."

"But what will you do? the Little Soul asked, just a little nervously, "that will be so terrible?"

"Oh," replied the Friendly Soul with a twinkle, "we'll think of something."

Then the Friendly Soul seemed to turn serious, and said in a quiet voice, "You are right about one thing, you know."

"What is that?" the Little Soul wanted to know.

"I will have to slow down my vibration and become very heavy to do this not-so-nice thing. I will have to pretend to be something very unlike myself. And so, I have but one favor to ask of you in return."

"Oh, anything, anything!" cried the Little Soul, and began to dance and sing, "I get to be forgiving, I get to be forgiving!" Then the Little Soul saw that the Friendly Soul was remaining very quiet.

"What is it?" the Little Soul asked. "What can I do for you? You are such an angel to be willing to do this for me!"

"Of course this Friendly Soul is an angel!" God interrupted. "Everyone is! Always remember: I have sent you nothing but angels."

And so the Little Soul wanted more than ever to grant the Friendly Soul's request. "What can I do for you?" the Little Soul asked again.

"In the moment that I strike you and smite you," the Friendly Soul replied, "in the moment that I do the worst to you that you could possibly imagine—in that very moment. . ."

"Yes?" the Little Soul interrupted, "yes. . . ?"

The Friendly Soul became quieter still.

"Remember Who I Really Am."

"Oh, I will!" cried the Little Soul, "I promise! I will always remember you as I see you right here, right now!"

"Good," said the Friendly Soul, "because, you see, I will have been pretending so hard, I will have forgotten myself. And if you do not remember me as I really am, I may not be able to remember for a very long time. And if I forget Who I Am, you may even forget Who You Are, and we will both be lost. Then we will need another soul to come along and remind us both of Who We Are."

"No, we won't!" the Little Soul promised again. "I will remember you! And I will thank you for bringing me this gift—the chance to experience myself as Who I Am."

And so, the agreement was made. And the Little Soul went forth into a new lifetime, excited to be the Light, which was very special, and excited to be that part of *special* called Forgiveness.

And the Little Soul waited anxiously to be able to experience itself as Forgiveness, and to thank whatever other soul made it possible.

And at all the moments in that new lifetime, whenever a new soul appeared on the scene, whether that new soul brought joy or sadness—and *especially* if it brought sadness—the Little Soul thought of what God had said.

"Always remember," God had smiled, "I have sent you nothing but angels."

Dear Parents,
    and All Lovers of Children:

    This wonderful story gives children a new way of looking at why "bad" things sometimes happen, and a new way of dealing with those things when they occur.

    The story also teaches that it is very okay to consider youself special, and to let others know just how special we all are.

    Finally, the story shows that everyone is loved by God in the same way, and that even people we may not consider to be our friends may be God's angels in disguise, sent to us to bring us a gift—the gift of growing in tolerance and understanding and forgiveness, and a chance to be who we really are.

    This parable first appeared in a slightly different form in the adult book *Conversations with God, Book 1,* and has been retold in cities across the country where I have been invited to lecture or offer pulpit talks at church services. I have re-created it as a children's book with color illustrations in response to the comment of countless people who have written to me, or stopped me after my talk, to say that it would "make a perfect children's story."

    I believe this parable came directly from God, and I know that any child who becomes familiar with it will be blessed by it. Thank you for loving children enough to bring them this story.

Neale Donald Walsch
Ashland, Oregon
January 1998

Thank you for reading *The Little Soul and the Sun*. Hampton Roads is pleased to offer our readers the Young Spirit line of books. Young Spirit books give children the extraordinary opportunity to begin exploring their spiritual nature from their toddler years all the way into their teens through lavishly illustrated picture books and finely crafted novels from award-winning authors.

Hampton Roads is also proud to publish more than a dozen of Neale Donald Walsch's most popular titles, including the Little Soul's sure-to-please second act: *The Little Soul and the Earth*.

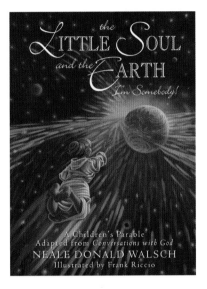

The Little Soul and the Earth is a delightful, vividly told and illustrated tale from the team that created *The Little Soul and the Sun*. The first of a new series of Little Soul adventures, it exemplifies the vital truth that God is with us always no matter where our own adventures lead and no matter how many times we may forget that truth. Gently reminding us that beauty and love are all around, the world of the joyous Little Soul is a place your child will want to visit again and again.

The Little Soul and the Earth: I'm Somebody!
A Children's Parable Adapted from *Conversations with God*
Written by Neale Donald Walsch
Illustrations by Frank Riccio

Picture Book / Ages 6–12 • Hardcover with dust jacket
32 pages • ISBN 978-1-57174-451-7 • $17.95

To see a complete list of our books for your Young Spirits
please visit us anytime on the Web: www.hrpub.com.

Young
Spirit
Books

Hampton Roads Publishing Company is dedicated to providing quality children's books that stimulate the intellect, teach valuable lessons, and allow our children's spirits to grow. We have created our line of Young Spirit books for the evolving human spirit of our children. Give your children Young Spirit books—their key to a whole new world!

HAMPTON ROADS PUBLISHING COMPANY
publishes books on a variety of subjects,
including spirituality, health, and other
related topics.

For a copy of our latest catalog,
call 978-465-0504 or
visit our website at www.hrpub.com